KV-061-577

DAD'S
CAMEL

TIGER series

DAD'S CAMEL

Joan Tate

Illustrated by
Helen Leetham

TIGERS

**A READ
ALONE BOOK**

Andersen Press · London

First published in 1990 by
Andersen Press Limited,
20 Vauxhall Bridge Road, London SW1

All rights reserved. No part of this publication may be
reproduced, stored in a retrieval system, or transmitted in
any form, or by any means, electronic, mechanical,
photocopying, recording or otherwise, without the
written permission of the publisher.

Text © 1990 by Joan Tate
Illustrations © 1990 by Andersen Press Limited

British Library Cataloguing in Publication Data
Tate, Joan, *1922-*
    Dad's camel.
    I. Title II. Leetham, Helen III. Series
    823′ .914 [J]

ISBN 0-86264-275-2

Typesetting by Print Origination (NW) Limited, Formby, Liverpool L37 8EG
Printed and bound in Great Britain by Courier International Limited
Tiptree, Essex

Dad brought it back.

It was one of those grey mornings in the Easter holidays. Dad was having a week off work and Ant and I were at home, both of us grumbling because there was nothing much to do.

'Play house with me,' said Ant.

'No,' I said.

Ant is only six and is always wanting to play house. Her name is Anita, but she's always called Ant.

'Well, let's go to the park,' she said.

'No.'

'Why not?'

I didn't like going off to the park with Ant. They let her go there as long as I was with her. But they wouldn't let her go alone. So I was always being lumped with her, and it meant she had to watch me playing football with the others, or I had to go with her to the swings.

'It's too wet,' I said.

'It's not raining,' said Ant, standing up and looking out of the window. 'Anyhow, here's Dad back again.'

She stood staring out of the window. Usually she goes tearing off to the door when she's seen him coming, but this time she didn't. She just stood there and said without turning round:

'And he's got a camel with him.'

I snorted. Just like Ant. She's nuts sometimes. Perhaps most sisters are, but she's not as crazy as some girls. But camels. I ask you.

'Go on,' I said. 'And sixty-four monkeys, I suppose.'

'He has, he *has*! Come and look for yourself.'

She had her nose flat against the glass as usual.

I didn't shift an inch because I know Ant. I've been had by her before, making up nutty stories and dragging me into them, then laughing her head off when I've believed her.

'He's bringing it into the front garden.'

'Oh, yeah.'

'It's eating the wallflowers.'

'Huh! Camels don't eat wallflowers.'

'This one does.'

I couldn't help it. I had to go and look. Ant hadn't moved and she wasn't laughing at all. She was pop-eyed and her nose was flatter than ever against the glass; her mouth, too, making the

glass steamy all round.

There *was* a camel in our front
garden, and it *was* eating the
wallflowers. Or rather, it was trying to.
Dad had a rope round its neck and he
was trying to get it *off* the wallflowers.
No wonder. We all knew about those

wallflowers. He knew Mum would be furious. The front garden was hers and the back garden was Dad's.

I couldn't find anything to say. My eyes popped, too, in fact nearly fell out altogether.

'It *is* a camel!' I said idiotically.

'I told you so,' said Ant – her favourite remark. 'You never believe anything I say.'

Then she came to life. She turned away from the window and ran for the door.

'I'm going to see. Dad might want me to help him.'

I followed her, trying not to hurry. When I looked back at the window, I saw that Dad had managed to get the camel's head up and the camel was looking straight through the window, straight at me.

There are some animals you can't really believe in when you actually see them. I think a camel is one of those. This camel stared at me with great round sad eyes, then it smiled. I know, I know, camels don't smile. But this one did, it really did. It had a great big mouth, like a clown's – big and loose and rubbery, and its smile was rather like a clown's, too – sad-funny. The

camel had a yellow wallflower hanging
out of one corner of its mouth as well,
so it looked quite foolish. Its teeth were
yellow. I rushed out after Ant.

She was already asking questions.

'Where did you get it from, Dad?

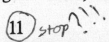

Whose is it? Can I hold it? Can we keep it? What's its name?'

I noticed Dad was looking rather worried. Ant wasn't going all that close, either, I noticed. In fact she was keeping well away, standing over by the corner of the house, one hand on the wall, ready to scoot back inside if anything happened.

I looked at Dad again. He was holding the rope and I think he was going to try to lead the camel round the back, because he was looking down the path which runs down the side of our house, the path that goes past the back door – to see if Mum was around, I suppose.

I was right.

'Where's your mother?' he said.

'She's not at work today? You know that. She's only gone out shopping.'

Dad looked relieved.

'Here,' he said. 'Hold this rope for a moment, will you?'

'Okay,' I said.

I'm eight, nearly nine, and a lot taller than Ant, but even then, the camel did make me feel rather small. It just stood there, and when Dad handed the rope over to me, it just looked down it's nose at me and snorted.

'Pffumpff.'

'Hang on a minute, and I'll fix something round the back.'

Dad went down the side path and Ant went after him, leaving me with the camel. I think Ant was scared. So was I, a little. There I was, left with a camel, in our own front garden, and the very moment they disappeared round the house, the camel started on the wallflowers again.

'No,' I said as firmly as I could. 'They're Mum's. Geddup.'

I yanked it away from the precious wallflowers, and to my surprise the camel raised its head and looked straight at me again, just as it had

13

through the window, with those sad brown eyes. It seemed to be saying it was hungry and couldn't I do something about it? It *was* a small camel, compared with the ones you see in zoos, and those great creatures racing about deserts on television. But in our front garden, it seemed to take up an awful lot of space.

I looked down at its feet. They were huge, like a giant dog's, but with only two toes. Its legs were very knobbly and didn't look as if they could ever win a race.

Dad came back. Thank goodness.

'Come on,' he said, jerking his head the way he had come. 'We'll park him out at the back for the moment. The tree's strong enough.'

He turned to go, so I followed. At least, I followed as far as the rope would go, and then I had to stop.

'Come on!' yelled Dad.

'Come *on*,' yelled Ant from a safe

distance.

'Come on,' I yelled at the camel. 'Move!'

The camel stood and stared.

I yanked again. I tugged and tugged. I hauled at the rope, then jerked it so that the camel's head wobbled for a moment. But it didn't budge. It didn't move its feet one inch. Dad started laughing.

'Here,' he said.

Like lightning, he had bent down and pulled a whole wallflower plant out by the roots. He had taken it from the end of the row and you could see the earthy patch where it had been. I suppose he thought Mum wouldn't notice just one gone, especially at the end of the row, while one from the middle she would have noticed at once.

Dad waved the wallflower under the camel's nose. It opened its mouth and made a stab at it, but Dad was quicker and took a step back, still holding out

the wallflower. That was how we got it
down the side path, Dad walking
backwards waving a wallflower, letting
the camel have a nibble now and again,
not too much, but just enough so that it
wanted some more, the camel following

16

slowly. And me, nipping along between
them with the rope in my hand, trying
to get out of the way of those great
spongy feet.

Dad got the camel all the way down
to the bottom of the garden and there

he tied it to the tree which holds up the other end of the washing line. Just in time. Because the wallflower was finished. It wasn't a very big tree, but neither was the camel all that big, and anyhow the tree was stronger than the post the other end.

'Where did you get it, Dad?' said Ant, hopping up and down with excitement, but still at a safe distance away, I noticed. 'Where did you get it? Is it ours? Can we keep it? Did you buy it for us? How much was it?'

'I won it in a bet,' said Dad. 'I don't know what your mother's going to say.'

I thought I knew.

'Pffumpff,' said the camel.

Mum came back about half an hour later. By that time, we had got our heads together and had made a plan.

'Where will it sleep?' said Ant.

'Haven't time to think about that yet,' said Dad. 'We could clear the shed, perhaps?'

'Mum would be pleased,' I said.

Mum was always on about all the junk in the shed.

'True,' said Dad, thoughtfully.

'And what does it eat?' said Ant.

Ant is always asking questions before you've had time to think anything out.

'Well, there's plenty of grass and stuff about, isn't there?' said Dad. Then he smiled. 'Mum would be pleased about that, too, wouldn't she?'

I grinned at Dad and he grinned back. Dad wasn't all that keen on gardening, so the back garden didn't look like the front garden. In fact, the back garden was a wild jungle of weeds and grass and a few old gone-to-seed cabbages, with the washing line strung along the path.

'Does it bite?' said Ant.

'Not if you're nice to it. It's only a young one.'

'How do you know?'

'Well, it's not very big, is it? Its hump hasn't grown much yet. That's what the bloke said.'

'What bloke?'

'The bloke I won it off. He said it's only young and wouldn't take much feeding and only a bucket of water to drink now and again.'

'Now and again? What does that mean?'

'Well, we'll see.'

'Where did he get it from?'

'I don't know. He had it there in the pub yard. We had a bet on it. And I won.'

We had gone back into the kitchen and were looking at the camel out through the kitchen window. Dad had brewed a cup of tea. The day wasn't nearly so grey and dull as it had been a little while ago.

The camel was standing by the tree gazing all round it. It looked a bit of a dope, because of those eyes. It was a brownish-greyish colour and its tail was like a silly bit of thick string with a tuft on the end of it. It wiggled quite a lot.

'Do they really keep water in that hump for weeks and weeks on end?' I said. I remembered reading about camels going for days in deserts without any water.

'Expect so,' said Dad, sipping noisily at his tea.

He didn't sound all that certain to me.

Then Mum came in. She walked straight in through the back door and thumped her plastic carriers down on the kitchen table.

'Someone's pulled up one of my wallflowers,' she said, at once. 'Right at the end. Near the side path. Was it one of you two?'

Ant shook her head and started giggling.

'Not me,' I said.

'What's the matter with you?' said Mum crossly. She took off her jacket, hung it up on the hook on the back door then turned back to us. 'It's no laughing matter,' she went on. 'I suppose you're going to tell me it was your dad?'

'It wasn't me,' said Ant.

'Nor me,' I said.

'Nor me,' said Dad. That wasn't really true, but although he had actually pulled it up, he hadn't eaten it.

'The CAMEL took it,' yelled Ant suddenly, as if she couldn't possibly keep it to herself any longer.

'Camel? What camel, silly?'

Ant is so used to being told she's silly

22

that she doesn't even bother to answer, but this time she did.

'I'm not silly,' she said.

Dad hadn't said anything except 'nor me' yet. He was leaning against the sink unit, looking out of the window and then back at Mum. Then he laughed again.

'That's right,' he said. 'Ant's not at all silly this time. Take a look out there.'

Mum went over to the sink and looked straight out into the garden. We all held our breaths and waited.

It was very, very quiet.

Mum closed her eyes and kept them closed.

'Did I see something?' she said.

'Yes!' yelled Ant, leaping up and down. 'A camel!'

Mum opened her eyes again. I watched her. She turned slowly round and looked at Dad. Then she looked out of the window again.

'And where, may I ask,' she said very slowly, 'did you find *that*?'

'Dad won it,' I said. 'He won it, and so it's ours. I mean Dad's. We can keep it in the shed, can't we? And it can eat all that grass, can't it? And it only drinks water. Then the shed would be cleared out, wouldn't it? And the grass would be got rid of, wouldn't it? That's what you've always wanted, isn't it?'

I stopped.

Mum turned right round and looked at us one by one, first Dad, then me, then Ant. I could hardly keep my face straight, because Mum would've been furious if she thought we were making fun of her.

'You *have* got it all worked out, haven't you?' she said. 'A *camel*. You just can't keep a camel in a garden that size.'

'Why not?' I said.

'You just can't. People don't.'

'Dad could.'

Mum looked at Dad.

I could see there might be going to be a huge row. I could see she didn't know whether to laugh or cry, be cross with Dad, or furious with us all. I saw her face wobbling about for a moment, and then she turned and looked out of the window again.

The camel was chewing away at some grass round the tree, tearing out great chunks, then just munching. Then it raised its head and started nibbling at the lower branches of the tree. Its long neck stretched out almost straight and

its great rubbery lips folded their way
round leaves, then with a jerk it pulled
its head back and the bunch of twigs
and leaves came off the tree and the
camel stood there munching and
munching, leaves flicking round and
twigs disappearing as it turned to face
the house, its eyes staring solemnly.

Mum was leaning over the sink, too,
now, her face quite close to the window,
and when the camel saw her staring at
it, it nodded in a friendly sort of way,

twigs and leaves sprouting in all directions out of its mouth. It seemed to be smiling at the same time.

Mum couldn't help it.

She laughed.

Then she looked at Dad again, and they both began laughing, leaning against the sink and not even looking at us.

'Give me that cup of tea,' she said at last, when she could speak again. 'If anyone needed a cup of tea, I do.'

We all had another cup of tea with her, even Ant, who usually just has a milky mixture to be like everyone else. Dad told Mum how he had won the camel, and just hadn't known what to do with it. So he had brought it home.

'If you think I'm going to feed a camel as well as you lot, then you've got another think coming,' said Mum.

'We'll feed it,' I said. 'Won't we, Dad?'

Dad nodded.

'We'll have to. You can't just leave camels lying about in back gardens without feeding them,' he said.

As if it had heard what Dad said, the camel suddenly lay down on the ground. Its knobbly legs just folded awkwardly under it and it kind of collapsed in a heap, a yellowish-brownish-greyish heap of camel on the ground, its nose in the air, its eyes half-closed, its small ears twitching and flapping.

Mum opened the window.

'I've never seen anything like it before,' she said.

'Pffumpff,' said the camel.

'Humph,' said Mum. 'I can see nothing but trouble coming. But it does look rather like your cousin Cyril, I must say.'

So we called it Cyril.

I wanted it to be Lancelot. I don't know why, but the camel looked as if it

28

had a rather grand name like Lancelot. Sort of noble. Ant wanted to call it Cammie, a silly name, I thought, but she just went on calling it Cammie. But Mum and Dad called it Cyril, and that was two against my one, so Cyril it became.

We set to work at once.

Dad found some old plastic sacks that had been in the shed for years, and some paper sacks he'd been saving for something and had never used. Just like Dad.

'You start collecting up some grass and fill those,' he said. 'Here's one for you, Ant, and two for you, Den.'

Ant took her sack off, dragging it behind her, and started stuffing handfuls of grass into it at a great rate. That would keep her quiet for hours. I wasn't so keen.

'Can't you cut the grass first?' I said. 'It's hard work pulling it up like this. It'll take hours to fill a sack.'

So Dad got out his old billhook he uses sometimes when the weeds get so high the neighbours complain, and he started slashing away in fine style. We soon had a whole lot of cut grass lying there and we could actually see the fence at the bottom of the garden.

The camel just watched us. Dad started doing the shed. He was chucking things out through the door and whistling loudly, so the camel was most interested in him. The shed is against the bottom fence and isn't very big, but it certainly looked a lot bigger when Dad had emptied it.

'Will it fit inside?' I said.

'Let's try, shall we?' said Dad. 'Come on, Cyril my lad.'

He untied the rope from the tree and tugged the camel towards the shed. Cyril put on one of his I'm-not-budging stunts again, his long neck stretching farther and farther out, but his feet not moving. They looked bigger than ever.

'Shall I get another wallflower?'

'Better not, with Mum watching,' said Dad. 'She'd skin us alive. Try a dandelion or two.'

There were plenty of those, so I pulled up two huge ones and held them under Cyril's long nose. He sniffed at them and wrinkled his nose and lips in disgust, like an enormous guinea pig, then suddenly he grabbed the lot out of my hand and started munching again. He dribbled, too. And an awful lot. But he didn't move from the spot.

'Try putting a whole heap inside the shed,' said Dad.

We did just that, putting a whole sackful inside the shed as far away from the door as possible. I held dandelions out in front of him until he took a few steps towards the shed, and slowly we got him near the door.

Then he stopped again, right in the doorway.

'Watch out for those back legs,' said

Dad. 'I've heard they kick, and look at those great feet.'

I wondered where he'd heard that.

Cyril was just a little shorter than the doorway, as long as he kept his head down. He didn't. He poked his head inside the door once, and sniffed. Then he pulled his head out and rested his chin, if you could call it a chin, on the tin roof above the door.

'Pffumpff,' he said, scratching his chin in a dreamy kind of way, swaying back and forth so that the roof did the scratching for him.

But he didn't budge his feet.

We all stood around watching him. It was almost as good as a show.

'Go *in*, Cammie,' said Ant fiercely, stamping her foot.

Cyril turned his head and glared at her. She took a quick step backwards.

'Go in, go in, go IN!' she cried, rather squeakily this time.

'Pffumpff.'

And believe it or not, the camel went into the shed.

Even Mum came out to look, and we all stood round the door gazing at Cyril's tail, which wiggled back at us. The camel could just get inside. It was eating the dandelions and gazing back at Mum through the small window in the side.

'Well, I suppose that's one way of keeping the weeds down,' she said. 'And how is it going to get out?'

As if in answer to her question, Cyril began to turn round in the shed. There

wasn't really quite enough room, but he managed. I saw the shed bulging a little and wondered what would happen when Cyril grew a bit bigger.

'We'll need another shed soon,' said Ant. 'That one doesn't fit very well.'

Dad had closed the door as soon as Cyril had started turning round. The door was in two halves, like a stable door, so that was just right. The camel got its head out of the top and looked at all of us for a change. Up to now, we had been doing all the looking at *him*.

'I don't know,' said Mum, shaking her head. 'What are we going to do about it? What use is a creature like that? You can't eat it and it doesn't even lay eggs.'

'Well, it's done something for your roses, anyhow,' said Dad.

It was true. Cyril had left a steaming heap under the tree. Even Mum couldn't complain about that. She's always saying the soil in the town is no good for growing things and what the garden needed was a good load of farmyard manure for her roses.

You can tell Mum was brought up on a farm. But there aren't any farms for miles around here, so the camel had been some help. Mum whipped the spade away from against the shed and scooped the heap straight up, then went off towards the front garden and her precious roses.

Dad blew his nose like a trumpet.

'Now, you two,' he said. 'We've got a

camel in the shed. Mum's in the front,
happy for her roses for the moment. So
what about raking up this lot and filling
up the rest of the sacks?'

'I'm tired,' said Ant.

'You talk to Cyril, then,' said Dad.
'Den and I'll do this.'

'His name's Cammie,' said Ant. 'Isn't
it, Cammie?'

The camel looked down at her.

'Pffumpff.'

'There,' said Ant. 'I told you.'

She moved a little nearer. Now that the camel was actually inside, she was braver. She held up a bunch of grass. The camel at once snatched it from her and gobbled it up in about two munches. Ant got another bunch. It gobbled that, too.

'Cammie's hungry,' she said.

'I have a nasty feeling camels eat a lot,' said Dad. 'But there's enough to keep it going for the moment, so we'll worry about that tomorrow.'

I went to fetch some water for the camel. I got the red plastic bucket and filled it almost to the top. It was heavy to carry, and I only just made it down the path. By the time I got down there, Dad had cleared almost the whole patch at the bottom of the garden, and the camel was lying down.

I put the bucket down and looked over the edge of the door. The camel at once got up again and the shed heaved. I opened the door and put the bucket

down just inside it.

Almost before I had closed the door behind me, there was a great slurping, sloshing, sucking, slobbery noise and then the bucket came flying out over the door.

Cyril wanted some more.

He drank three full buckets that night, and by tea time, we were all rather tired, what with fetching and carrying and cutting grass and filling sacks.

But the day had gone like lightning.

Of course, it's hard to keep something like a camel in your garden a secret for any length of time. In fact, we couldn't keep it a secret at all.

The neighbours knew. They couldn't help it, because they could actually see it. There's a fence down one side of the garden and that's not very high. And down the other side there's a hedge. So there was a lot of chat over the hedge and the fence as the next-doors came to see what on earth was going on.

And now that we'd cleared the tall
grass and weeds at the bottom, our back
neighbours could see the garden for the
first time for ages. And we could see
them.

When the milkman came the next
morning, we could hear him whistling
as usual, and the clink of bottles, then
there was an awful crash. We all rushed
to the back door, and saw at once that

he had dropped two bottles of milk on to the path.

'Thought I saw a camel,' he said to Mum.

'You did,' she said.

'Thought I was seeing things,' said the milkman.

'You were,' said Mum.

She cleared the mess up and the milkman gave us two more bottles, then went off muttering about his accounts being in a right old muddle now.

'Camels,' he said as he went off. 'Some people!'

We were suddenly very popular.

The neighbours kept dropping in to borrow some sugar, or something. Or to ask after Gran, who wasn't at home anyhow. She'd gone to stay with our Uncle Jack. Even the neighbours who'd complained about the weeds became quite friendly. Though perhaps that was because of the weeds disappearing all in one day.

Ant and I showed everyone the
camel. Mum was already fed up with so
many people coming and going, and
Dad had gone to the library to find out
about camels.

The camel didn't seem to mind. It
just stood there, outside the shed now,
tied to the tree, munching. It seemed to
be able to munch for ever.

Dad had fastened another rope round
its head now, like a halter on a horse.
Then he tied a longer rope to the halter
and the tree. That meant the camel
could eat a wider circle and he was
doing quite well on the hedge, too.

'Where did you get it?' said John,
who is at school with me and lives three
doors down the road.

I could see he was envious. Nothing
like this had ever happened to him.

'Dad brought it back yesterday,' I
said, as if Dad brought things like
camels back every day.

'Are you going to keep it?'

'Of course.'

'Wish I had one.'

Ant and Liz, John's sister, were standing staring at the camel.

'Does it do as you tell it?' said Liz.

'Of course,' said Ant. 'Geddup, Cammie.'

Cyril had just started to lie down. But he stopped halfway and stood up again. Even Ant looked rather surprised.

'Pffumpff!' said Cyril, rather loudly.

Then he stretched his head down towards them.

Liz squealed and rushed away down the path. Of course she wasn't as used to camels as we were.

Ant simply pulled up another bunch of grass and dandelions and held it out. Cyril couldn't quite reach so took another step towards her, stretching his neck again.

That was when everything started to go wrong.

The rope snapped off over by the tree.

Cyril shook his head and the rope swung about.

Then he just strolled off towards the house.

Liz had been standing by the corner of the house. She squealed even more loudly than before and turned and ran down the side into the front garden.

Cyril seemed interested in the squeal, because he strolled over to the same corner and then down the side path. I could see him quite well from where I was standing.

When Cyril got to the back door, he stopped and looked inside.

Then he went inside.

Just disappeared. One moment he was there, his head inside the back door, and the next moment he had gone inside.

I looked at John.

John looked at me.

'It's gone inside,' said John.

'I can see that,' I said. 'Come on, or Mum'll be wild.'

We raced down the path and met Mum on the doorstep.

'What's going on?' said Mum. 'I thought I heard someone. What's all this noise about? Is it that dratted animal again?'

I stared at her.

Cyril, a whole camel, not a very big one, but a *camel* all the same, had just gone into our house.

And here was Mum, simply standing on the doorstep as if nothing had happened.

'Where is it?' I said.

'What?'

'The camel! Cyril!'

'What do you mean, where is it?' said Mum. 'Don't you know?'

I looked at John.

John looked back at me.

He's never much use when you're in a fix.

Liz came back from the front garden and Ant appeared from the back.

'It's in the house,' said Ant in her squeaky voice.

Mum turned round like lightning, as if she expected to see the camel just behind her.

'What do you mean, *in* the house?' she said.

'We saw it go in.'

'*In* the house. Inside?'

'Yes.'

Mum stood stock still for a moment, then sprang into action.

'Stay where you are, all of you,' she said. 'Except you, Den. You come with me.'

I went into the house with Mum.

When you go in through our back door down the side of the house, you turn left to go into the front room and right to go into the kitchen. You step straight into a sort of hall where we put our coats and things, and the stairs go

up from there.

Can a camel walk up stairs?

Well, this one could. We glanced into the front room and there was certainly no camel there.

It couldn't be in the kitchen or Mum would have noticed, wouldn't she?

So we went upstairs.

The bathroom is at the top of the stairs, you turn right and straight ahead of you is Mum and Dad's room, the biggest of the three. As soon as we got to the landing at the top, we knew the camel was there somewhere.

49

First there was the smell.

Secondly, we could see that string tail wiggling and twitching as it hung over the edge of Mum and Dad's bed.

Thirdly, there was another heap for the roses.

I looked into the room.

Cyril was lying down, on his side this time. His head was resting on Mum's dressing table. He looked very strange.

Perhaps he was ill? There was a kind of white foam all round his mouth and his eyes looked very droopy.

'My talc!' gasped Mum. 'It's eaten the lot.'

No wonder Cyril wasn't feeling too good.

It's one thing having a camel. It's another having a camel inside your house.

But it's quite another matter getting it out again. Especially when it doesn't want to go. Cyril clearly was staying where he was, and I must say he looked

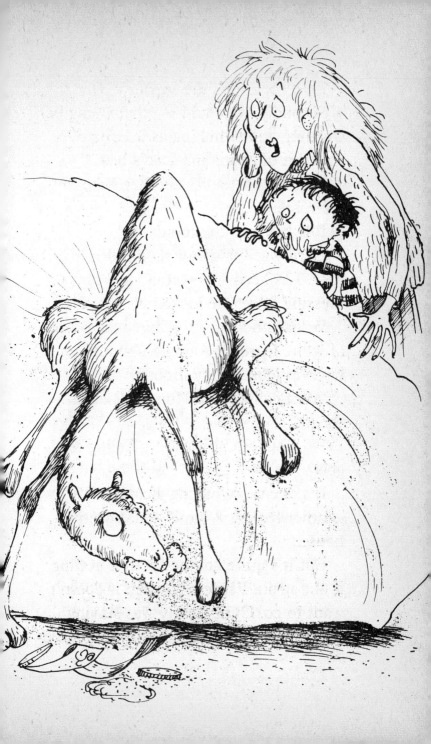

very comfortable indeed on Mum's quilt.

Mum decided.

She wasn't just cross. She was very angry. I think she was a bit scared, too, at the sight of her bedroom *full* of camel.

We went downstairs again, out into the garden, where the others were standing around waiting to see what would happen.

'Den,' said Mum. 'You know our phone's not working. Go down to the kiosk and phone the police. Dial 999. Ask for the police. Tell them where to come. John, go to the library and find Den's dad and tell him to come back. Ant, you and Liz go along to Liz's house and stay there until I come and fetch you.'

Ant didn't look at all pleased at the idea. But Mum was being the major-general in command of her troops, and when she uses that voice, you do as you're told.

So Ant went, dragging Liz with her.

I scooted off at once, and so did John.

There's a telephone kiosk down at the end of our road. I was quite excited. I dialled 999.

'Which service, please?'

I couldn't think what the voice meant at first.

'Do you want police, fire service or an ambulance?'

'Police,' I managed to say.

Before I could blink, a voice said:

'Police, here. Where are you ringing from?'

I gave them the name of our road.

'What's the trouble?'

'There's a camel in our house.'

'Do you know it's a very serious offence to abuse the emergency services?'

I didn't know what that meant. But I could tell that they didn't believe a word I was saying. After all, it was a bit like one of Ant's stories.

'It's true. It's true!' I shouted. 'Come and see! It's in our house and it's got upstairs and my mum told me to go and phone you. It's true.'

'Where are you?'

'In the kiosk at the end of the road.'

'Stay where you are until we come.'

'What? In the kiosk?'

'Yes.'

'All right.'

That's how I got a ride in a police car on the same day as a camel got into our house.

There was quite a crowd outside our house when we drove up in the police car. Everyone turned round to look at us when we got out. There was a policeman and a policewoman as well as the driver. And me.

Mum was standing there waiting, her arms folded.

'At last,' she said. 'I thought you were never coming.'

'They wouldn't believe me,' I said. 'I had to wait for them at the kiosk.'

'Well, it's true,' said Mum to the policeman. 'There's a camel up there in my bedroom, and would you please get it out.'

The police went into the house and Mum went in with them. They wouldn't let me come in, so we stood outside waiting. Then John and Dad turned up, puffing and panting. They'd run all the way.

'They're inside,' I said to Dad. 'With Mum.'

Dad didn't wait. He went inside, too.

'I had a ride in that car,' I told John.

'In the radio car? Go on.'

'I did.'

'Bet you didn't.'

'Come on, then.'

I dragged him over to the police car.

'Didn't I have a ride in your car?' I said to the driver.

He nodded.

'You certainly did.'

'There,' I said to John.

John had to believe me now, but he didn't want to. I suppose he thought it just wasn't fair, me having all the luck, a camel as well as a ride in a police car.

We seemed to wait an awful long time, but then the policeman came out and after he had spoken to the driver of the car, the driver spoke into a microphone for quite a while. The policewoman kept telling the people on the pavement to move along, which they did at first, but they soon drifted back. The news about the camel had got around, so lots of people started taking a little stroll our way.

'Den!'

It was Dad.

'The camel's at the top of the stairs,' said Dad, 'and no one can get past it. They've sent for someone to help. Now they want someone up there, and no one can get through the bathroom window. It's the only one open.'

'Me?'

'You're the only one small enough to get in that way.'

Dad got the ladder and propped it up. I climbed up, with Dad following up behind me and someone standing on the bottom rung.

The bathroom window is very small, the kind with a hatch window at the top. That part was open. I unhitched the bar and with Dad pushing me from behind and me wriggling, I went head first into the bathroom. Once I'd got my hands on to the top of the lavatory cistern, Dad let go.

The bathroom looked quite different from up there. I managed to get down without breaking my neck, though a few things got knocked to the floor. Then I opened the door.

It was quite a shock.

The camel was lying at the top of the stairs, its head facing down, its tail and backside against the bathroom door. It looked enormous and the smell was awful.

I looked over it and could see several people down below, including Mum.

'Give it a thump on the back,' said the policeman. 'See if it'll get up.'

I touched Cyril's back. It was soft and hairy. It was the first time I had actually touched him. Somehow I'd thought he would be bristly, but he wasn't. Cyril raised his head a little, then lowered it again.

'Thump it,' said the policeman again.

I gave Cyril a slap and dust flew up into my face, but Cyril took no notice at all. I slapped a bit harder, but that just raised more dust.

Then someone else came into the house downstairs. A man in ordinary clothes. He came straight up the stairs and started talking to Cyril in a quiet voice, and Cyril began to take some notice, shifting about a bit and showing signs of life.

The man looked up to where I was standing in the bathroom doorway.

'Can you see the tail?' he said.

'Yes.'

'Well, take a hold of it and give it a little shake. Gently now.'

I bent down and touched Cyril's tail. The whole great camel body gave a shudder.

'Now shake it a bit more.'

I held on to that bit of old rope with a tuft on the end and gave it another shake.

Cyril gave another shudder, bigger this time.

'Now,' said the man. 'I've got the halter rope. When I tell you to, give its tail a twist. Not too hard, mind you, just a little twist. So that it feels it. That's how I get it to get up when it's feeling lazy. It knows what it means.'

He had asked everyone to get out of the house, so the way out was clear.

'If it gets up, let the tail go at once,' said the man. 'Now, try.'

I gave Cyril's tail a little twist. He shifted and let out a grunt.

'Bit harder,' said the man.

I tried again.

There was an earthquake. Grunting and groaning and puffing and with awful rumbles from inside, Cyril got to his feet. He filled the whole landing now and I couldn't see any more.

Talking all the time, the man gradually persuaded Cyril to come down the stairs.

'Don't be frightened now. Come on, now. That's it. Take it easy. That's it. Come on then, Shalimah, come on. It's all right. Nothing to be frightened of. It's only me. You know me. Come on, then. That's it. Clever girl. Soon be all right. Clever girl, clever girl.'

Girl!

That's how they got the camel out of our house. The man was Cyril's keeper at a small private zoo outside town. The zoo had reported the lost camel to

the police, so someone had been ready
to come as soon as they found it.

Gradually everyone went away.

Gradually we got the mess cleared
up.

Dad had won Cyril from the man
who had first found him – eating his
way through *his* wallflowers. He'd been
only too glad to get rid of it.

One of the policemen wrote all this
down after the rest had gone. That took
a long time.

At last there was no one left in the
house but us. At last we got some tea.
Mum and Dad, Ant and me. No camel.

'No more camels brought back to this
house, thank you,' said Mum firmly.
'Or anything bigger than a guinea pig.'

'Couldn't happen again,' said Dad.
'But I couldn't just leave it there,
could I?'

'Yes, you could. They could have
fetched it from there.'

'But then *we* would never have had a

camel,' said Ant suddenly.

'And no one else here has ever had a camel in the garden before,' I said. 'Not to mention in the house.'

'No,' said Dad. 'It'll be quite something to tell them at school, won't it?'

Just what I was thinking.

And if the same thing happens to anyone else, then they know where to come for expert help, don't they?

Mum's roses are great this year.

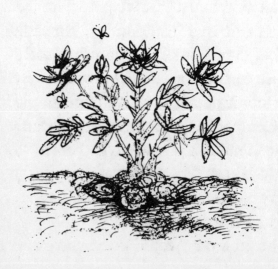